A Cautionary Covid-19 Tale

The takeaway had a sign in the window (which was fully covered in advertisements and the takeaway menu), "only one customer in the shop at any one time, wait til the ENTER sign lights". The ENTER sign was lit so he opened the door, went in and checked the menu on the wall.

After perusing the menu he placed his order and pulled out his card.

"Cash Only, we don't take cards, there is a cash machine next door"

He checked his wallet and had enough to pay for his meal, so handed over the notes and took the change.

"Thanks it'll be about twenty minutes, are you OK waiting"

"Yeah, no problem"

There were a few magazines on a small table in the seating area, mostly supermarket periodicals advertising food and meals to make, but he decided to see what was happening on his phone, the internet and news sites held a little more interest than the magazines.

He heard a noise but didn't take any notice, the BBC site had an article on Liverpool's lifting of the Premiership, and that now had all his attention.

The person who had served him had disappeared in the back, presumably getting his order together.

There were some more noises, like something scurrying on the floor and behind the seating .

"Maybe it's the heating"

His phone had his attention.

Then there was a bite on his ankle, it felt like a bite , he grabbed his ankle (he had come into the shop wearing a T-shirt , tracksuit bottoms and slippers , nothing else...

There was blood on his hands.

"What the .... "

He didn't finish the sentence ....

The server came back behind the counter, with the owner and looked at what was left of their customer.

"Are they all back in the box?"

"Yes"

"Well, that looks like enough mince to keep us going for the next fortnight......."

20-9

In my pocket I keep a chain with a heart shaped locket, inside is a picture which may have been my wife, daughter , mother , I don't know , but I keep it to remember there was a real past, and they never noticed I still had it.

I really never thought it would matter, I didn't bother voting in the last election but knew that everything would stay as it was and we would get the same bunch that were usually voted in time after time. Anyway no one would vote for a party who's main platform was the abolition of all political parties (apart from themselves) and stood as The Party. That would never happen would it? That is what the whole country thought, but the mainstream and social media posts along with other "sweeteners" such as implementations of a rigid caste system based on religion and skin colour, complete lockdown of immigration and purging or "undesirables" resulted in a landslide victory for The Party.

When they took to power all other political members who were not their members were jailed and replaced by designated members of The Party. That was the result of the final election in our country. The Party declared there would be no need for elections going forward.

The next phase was to dissolve the judiciary and apply working groups to dispense "justice" as The Party saw fit.

We shouldn't have been surprised, the world only had on commercial entity The Corporation which came into being by aggressive mergers and takeovers and now controlled the world's media and production and could therefore direct electorates (where they still existed) to vote for what they decided.

The Corporation also owned the governments and ruling parties. A Corporation only serves itself.

When The Party took control , for economic efficiency they dispensed with wages, and there was no action that anyone could take.

Schools were also terminated as The Party determined that for the nation to be as productive as possible our population could start to be used from the age of five.

Anyone who appeared to dissent was seldom seen the following day , so people kept quiet.

The population was supplied with basic sustenance , just enough to keep the workforce alive and productive where required , although shops no longer existed, again there was no requirement for them.

And now there is one newspaper that tells us how good our lives are and how the country is improving , and one TV channel that tells the same. I seem to remember before when we have lots of newspapers and more that one TV channel , although we have been told that is a fallacy.

Libraries now only carry one book and todays newspaper, and again I am sure I remember when there were lots of books, but I am probably wrong.

And I thought I never saw this coming. I did what I was told, well what the papers and TV told me and I was promised a perfect life free from foreign influences and I would have all that I want.

I can hardly sleep now. I know I have to start work at six and will be back in my cubicle at eight , that is fourteen hours seven days a week. I work one week digging holes and then one week filling them in . I don't know what it is for but I am told it is the greater good. I know that if I question why I am doing this I may not see another day.

If I do what I am told the country will benefit , The Party tells me but in a world where no children are seen to be born , and a nation whose only purpose is to work , there is no personal future. Life is reduced to a series of repeated tasks with no personal satisfaction and no way out …. ever!!!

But there is still the slightest sliver of hope as I clutch the chain of my heart shaped locket and know there was a past, and hope there will be a future.

... and brown paper

Two wait at a bus stop

They are waiting , maybe for a bus , maybe for another , maybe fro a break in the weather , it is raining.

The bus stop is sheltered enclosed on three sides , with a seat running the full length, and therefore offering some shelter

The two men stand either side of the bus stop , masked , as the plague is still rampant so you don't want to spread it, but cannot trust strangers.

In the centre of the seat is a package, possibly a box wrapped securely in featureless brown paper.

Is that yours?

No, Is it yours?

No

Should we see what's inside it?

It might be someone's who left it here while he went for some cigarettes , matches or just for a pee

It must not be valuable then

It could be dangerous

What do you mean?

It could be a bomb , or contain poison

But it's at a bus stop, and one that is seldom used

And the bus is very late, it might be cancelled

They're always doing that

The bus services these days are so unreliable

Should we hand it to the bus driver , if amd when it comes?

Like I said , it might be dangerous , that would not be a good idea.

Is there any writing on it? Or a label or something

I can't see anything

Pick it up carefully and look

No you do it , it's your idea

Have you got any gloves

No but I have an Aldi carrier bag , would that help?

I suppose so , give it to me

He examines the package , back and bottom , there is nothing written on , nothing sealing it either , no Sellotape or tabs

----

There's a smell of vinegar , vinegar and brown paper , like the Jack and Jill nursery rhyme

I had some fish and chips in it last night , the vinegar is probably from them

I think we should open it , see what's inside

No, no , what if the owner comes along and it;s something personal?

Well if it's important , you don't leave it unattended in a remote deserted bus shelter

And where is that bus , it's got very dark very quickly , and there;s not been any traffic along here, in fact there's not been any people walking past , it's like we are the last people on earth . That's a joke.

Is it , I am getting worried about this , Im sure there were shops , but I can't see anything down the road. It's so dark I don't think we could safely leave this bus stop

Oh come on the bus will be here soon

What time is it?

There's something wrong, my watch says twelve o' clock , and it;s stopped

So does mine , this is scaring me.

I can't see across the road , it's like the darkness is drawing in on us.

What is is in the package?

Well it's us , the bus stop and the package , we need to know

Slowly unwrapping the package , they found it contained a white box , upon opening the box they took out two tickets which read ; "One Passenger: Limbo"

The bus drew up and they joined with their tickets

....
....

Newspaper Article: Two gentlemen were found dead in the bus stop on XXXXXXX street. Foul play is not suspected, they had no families.

In The Flat Field

I often go out for walks on my own, it helps me think and keeps my body in reasonable shape. A doctor recently said of me in a letter to my GP "Eyeballing him , he looks really fit", not sure if that was a reference to my fitness , physique or he just fancied me.

I decided to leave the road and go overland, and eventually came to a field. I thought it was odd because it was big but looked perfectly square , the hedges were a good six feet high and fairly solid , you could not see daylight through them at all, but that was fine, as I alighted from the style in the corner.

In the centre of the field was a patch of red , possibly roses or something but there seem to be some rodents going across the field to the red centre then going back out and disappearing into the thick hedges.

I noticed there seemed to be a path round the field , well the grass as a slightly different shade of green to the inner square.

I stepped into the inner square and one of the creatures skipped over my foot and into the hedge. I then noticed that I was on another path , about eighteen inches wide and realised that the field was in fact a series on concentric squares (can you say that about squares , I've only used it before about circles).

I then decided to go back to the outer path , but I couldn't , it was like there was a glass wall up , except I had just walked into this path , maybe there was a gap and I had been luck (or unlucky enough to find it. Working my way back I could not find a way thorough , though the creatures seemed to have no problem scuttling across the field.

Maybe there was a gap under the barrier that I could squeeze through. I touched and felt down with my hands but there was no way through, and as I was feeling a red mawed creature skipped past my fingertips through to the hedge , but it was like a brick wall to me.

I wondered if this was some kind of maze and did I have to go to the centre to find my way out, though I was apprehensive as the creatures were not being stopped but I was.

I took a deep breath and moved to the next path , sure enough I couldn't move back. I was concentrating more on where I had come from , rather than where I was going. I felt along this barrier but there was no way back, and still the creatures were able to move freely across the field, and I was not.

The only way I could go was toward the cluster of red roses at the centre of the field.

I stepped on to another path , I hadn't realised but the paths were getting narrower, I could feel the barrier almost physically pushing me towards the centre. This square was small enough for me to explore the whole of the barrier. There was no way out for me and there were more and more creatures emerging from the hedges.

I was getting scared, I then thought , my mobile phone which I took out but there was zero signal. I smashed my hands against the barrier ending up with bloodied knuckles, then a creature lunged at my bloodied have and bit me , I shook it off but knew I

MIKE SINGLETON

was being stalked.

I was being pushed toward the centre

And I saw

They were not red roses

They were bloody human remains ……..

Masks Are Mandatory

In England it was fine, the government said you didn't need to wear a mask. Yes, virus infections were the highest in the world, but the government knew what they were doing, and he always voted for them just like his daily red top told him to.

But he was in Scotland now and waiting for a bus.

You had to wear a mask in a shop, a pub, or a restaurant. They were infringing his human rights, he shouldn't have to wear a mask, but knew that if he didn't, he would be hit with a huge fine (though he had no money really) or even jail, and then he would probably lose his job, so "When In Rome" or rather "When In Scotland".

He pulled out his paper mask as the bus rolled up. The doors opened and he got on wearing his mask.

You can't wear that on here

What, you are kidding me, I just bought this

Nope you can't wear your own mask

You have to wear an official tested mask, take one off the pile there

He took one and put it on, paid his fare, contactless of course and turned to walk up the bus.

Most of the seats were filled, everyone masked and either glazy eyed or asleep

He did find a double seat and sat himself down.

Damn he had forgotten his headphones, he checked his phone, no bars, no signal. That was Scotland for you, so nothing to listen to , couldn't even scan the net , make a call stream anything. He was cut off.

He was surprised that the only sound was the buses wheels on the road (it was electric of course) but no one was speaking, or snoring. No one was listening to music and no phones went off, if it wasn't for the sound of the wheels there would be no sound at all.

The fibres in the mask were annoying him, like they were insects crawling on the skin of his face, almost as though they were stinging him. It didn't really hurt but it was starting to get annoying.

He tried to pull it away but it was stuck. He couldn't get the mask off and he was starting to have difficulty breathing. He looked round at the other passengers. He decided to get up and get off the bus , but he couldn't move. He didn't remember putting the seat belt on but these modern Scottish buses had all mod cons , unlike the ones he was used to back in England.

His breathing was getting shallower, his breath shorter , he was fading , fading , fading.

The light was dying, he was going , he now knew why the passengers were so quiet, the only one still functioning was the driver.

The driver continued along the road, his passengers were quite, the way he expected and liked them. This was his final delivery of the day.

He turned the bus into to the depot under the sign that read

SOYLENT CORPORATION - SCOTTISH BORDERS BRANCH ....

The Invitation

It was just a card , standard postcard size , but very high quality.

The card was an invite , there was an address in a high class expensive part of the city, and an offer of substantial financial remuneration for an hour of his time. A two way conversation would be expected and would be held in the library.

The money would come in very useful, there were bills to pay. There was also a time to arrive and dress was expected to be formal, suit and tie. Tomorrow night at seven o' clock. He would have to walk, but that would be fine , it was on a private road and that would be difficult for a taxi.

So here he was walking up the street, it was foggy and he was fifteen minutes early , but in plenty of time. At the bottom of the stone steps, he walked up, he couldn't see any lights on but sounded the brass knocker which seemed to be inordinately loud.

He waited

Five minutes later he was shown into a dimly lit hallway. The person indicated for him to give him his overcoat then he led him into what he assumed was the library.

Again this was dimly lit , three walls of books stacked tightly in their cases to the ceiling with very few gaps, and one of those contained the entry door with books above the stone lintel. The fourth wall contained two smaller bookcases and a window looking out onto a park.

He was shown to a leather chesterfield chair and was opposite another, his host he assumed with a walnut table in between them. The library was dimly lit, his host seemed almost featureless, but welcomed him, but his eyes were drawn to the books in the room , every one seemed to be in a grey leather binding , unusual to a library to have all the book sin a uniform binding , and in the dim light he couldn't see any titles just maybe a dark image at the top of each book spine.

Would you prefer tea, coffee, or wine ?

Tea is fine, white no sugar.

Tea arrived in a pot, with a small jug of milk, tea was served and he drank.

The conversation was an almost hypnotic question and answer session and the longer it went on, the more he felt he was being watched or at least observed. He was questioned, he answered, but became increasingly disturbed but realised that he was unable to move.

He felt a dragging pain like nothing he had ever felt before, like his whole being was being ripped from his body.

He hadn't noticed the book on his host's lap.

The pain was worse, it hurt, he was in excruciating pain, then nothing.

He opened his eyes, or he thought he was opening his eyes, because the angle was so odd. He was looking across the table at his own immobile body, his face a rictus of pain and fear. He was looking at himself. Then he was being raised up and placed onto a bookshelf.

His soul was in the book and he was looking down on his body, he knew what those darknesses were at the top of the spines, they were faces and here to watch the next unsuspecting person to have their soul torn out and placed in this library of stolen souls.

We do really need to make some room , the shelves are getting full , everyone heard. But there was nothing they could do. They could not move or speak, they could only watch and listen, and no doubt eventually go completely insane.

The Everlasting Two Minutes

The queue for the bus at the Galleries was long , but it was the only bus I could get back home with. It was eight miles so walking wasn't an option and I don't drive now.

I looked at my watch , it was 5:36 , and looked at the electric sign board and it said the X1 was due in two minutes.

The queue was growing behind me, and there was nowhere to go or anything to do and it was only two minutes I had to wait.

It is strange when you are waiting for a bus or train how time often seems to grind to a halt, it is the same when you are at work , it is almost like the clock stops.

I looked at my watch , 5:36 , looked at the sign board , the X1 would be two minutes , it was like time had stopped. I was wondering if my watch had stopped (well actually it was my phone I was checking) but didn't want to leave the queue for fear of losing my place. I could not see another clock or time display , though I knew there were ones in the adjoining shopping centre and supermarket.

5:36 , the X1 will be two minutes

I was starting to get a little perturbed. Surely two minutes had passed , it felt like it , but my phone and the electric sign said otherwise. The people in the queue seemed to be Ok chatting , looking at their phones , reading papers and just waiting like I was.

I stayed where I was . We were waiting for a bus and we didn;t want to wait another hour for the next one . It was dark outside and the wind was blowing although it was actually quite warm and seemed to be getting warmer for some reason.

The lights flickered and then came back on , something was happening , but the bus wasn't here and my phone said 5:36 and the electric sign said the X1 will be here in 2 minutes.

No one else looked disturbed , so it was only me who was feeling it , or was it everyone and everyone was too scared to admit that they thought that the wheels of time had ground to a juddering halt. How do you say that to someone you don't know and who is just in a bus queue with you. They would probably think you were at least a tiny bit disturbed.

But we were waiting. When I started it was twilight outside, it was now pitch black, but the bus still wasn't here and my phone still said 5:36 and the electric sign still said the X1 will be here in 2 minutes.

Something was wrong.

But what?

I thought I felt the building shudder slightly but no one reacted , no one moved , they still waited . I tapped the shoulder of the man in front of me and asked him for the time. There was no movement , no reaction.

I tried to turn to ask the person behind me and suddenly I was unable to move, I was now very frightened. I shouted :

"Can somebody tell me the time?"

No one moved , no one answered

It was getting hotter , I could smell brimstone, or what I thought brimstone would smell like

Then the back wall collapsed, opening a fiery red tunnel

The line started to move slowly and I was moving along with it.

The realisation set in , time had stopped for everyone at 5:36 and we were not waiting for a bus, we were condemned to eternal hell fire

The Film

The rain , rain rained down as they looked for the one they had lost. There was an address but it was a long walk up a dark , dank muddy track , walled on either side with ancient stone green with old mould. They walked together until they came to the building at the end of the path with a single dark weather worn door. The house was two storeys, brick and from what they could see had no windows.

They had a torch and the beam on the walls reflected a sickly ominous green light

There was a rusty, but usable knocker which they used and knocked three times, loudly. The noise seemed far too loud for the knocker. The door had no handle , keyhole or any apparent opening method, and when they pressed it there was absolutely no give. It needed to be opened from the inside.

Silence

So the knocker was used again.

The rain still fell soaking their clothes.

They heard something

Was the door going to open? There was a scraping and the door opened on a long passage lit by low power bulbs along its length.

"Could you tell us if Frankie came here?"

"Come In, Come In"

"But can you tell us"

"Come , follow me"

We were very unsure and nervous but followed them down the passage.

We came to a small room containing a video camera, four chairs , a projector , and a dirty white sheet on the wall hanging from the ceiling

"Sit down, Sit down"

The were hand glasses of what looked like red wine

"Drink, drink"

While thinking they shouldn't they downed the wine in one, wanting to get on with what they had come for.

"Where is Frankie? We are very worried , we have been looking for them and found this card in their jeans pocket that were left on the floor"

The card had the address and a scrawled map of this place to make sure it was found.

"Frankie should not have left that, this is a secret place"

"But where is Frankie"

"In the Film"

"In the Film?"

"Yes, In The Film. it is why Frankie came , See"

The projector started to whirr , and on the wall we saw Frankie , grainy and blurred but it was Frankie , looking distressed. There was no sound except the whirr of the projector but it looked like Frankie was pleading "Help Me, Get Me Out"

"Where is Frankie , give them to us know or we will call the police"

"I think not"

Mobile phones were taken out, but there was no signal . They were cut off in a building with no windows , no connection to outside , and they hadn't told anyone they were coming

They were alone.

They tried to get up , but were then hit by the reality that the could not move, the wine must have been drugged, though they were fully awake , able to talk but unable to move.

"You won't get away with this"

"I already have , Frankie is now in The Film immortal and trapped, I now need to prepare two more films to save you two"

They then noticed against the wall hundreds of film reels. It then dawned on them that many of the disappearances reported in the local news could be traced to here, but now they knew they could do nothing about.

The video camera started , and Robin watched in horror as Kai's body began to fade , stolen by the video camera . It took less than five minutes.

"Would you like to see?"

Kai appeared on the sheet screaming for help , trapped in The Film

The projector stopped and the films were placed in the rack.

There was one more to record …………

Drained

It didn't help that I had just watched John Carpenter's "The Fog". I love his minimalist compositions and he has made some amazing horror films but I really had writing to finish , but was a little uneased by the fog or mist that was now covering the village pond, which the picture window in my office looked out on.

It was dark but the mist was almost shimmering and I started thinking I could see darkness in it , but again half expecting undead zombies to rise from the bottom was my overactive imagination cranking up a gear.

I had work to do but recently every time I wrote I was starting to feel a little more drained as though my keyboard was draining a little of my life force from me, but I obviously wasn't eating properly or wasn't getting enough sleep, MY doctor and friends keep telling me I need to look after myself, but I really do need to get this writing finished and off to my publisher or else I won't get paid and then I won't be able to eat or even power my computer , or content delivery device as Apple once described their iPads.

There was something wrong , but was it in here , out there or in my head. Every time I touched the keyboard I could feel my life draining from me , this was wrong. Could I use a pen and paper of the old typewriter , but no, they wanted an electronic digital copy.

I was starting to feel like Chuck from "Better Call Saul" . Was I allergic to electricity or electronic devices?

Back to my computer , another few words and then something floated to my desk , a few locks of my hair , my hair was dropping out, what the hell. I was feeling more tired but the hair was a shock. I wasn't sure where it had come from. I pulled a little at my hair , but it all seemed well rooted enough. I was half expecting it to come right out.

There is no way I could complete this , it was going to kill me , I may be imagining it , but feeling drained by my vampire keyboard and my hair falling out was not good at all, I could ask for an extension.

Then I heard something , it was water outside , something had come out of the pond but it looked like it was a ghost of fog and then there were two in my office. Seriously, what the hell?

They didn't speak , but instructed me to go back to the computer and start typing.

"You are now our sustenance, like the others before you…"

I'd wondered vaguely why the rent on this place had been so cheap, but not complained. I was a struggling freelance writer.

Back at the computer I started to type , the more I wrote , the worse I felt . The article developed slowly , but I had a nose bleed , and cuts were appearing. My fingertips were blue and bruised , there was blood on the keyboard , I was now bleeding from my eyes.

"Keep Typing, You are our sustenance"

I typed

I typed

I typed

===

OK we need to clean this mess up and get it back on the market.

They won't be happy if they don't have food , and if we don't give them something they might come for us.

How the hell did we get into this? I really want out , I hate it.

You know that's not an option , there's only one way out and you don't want that….

==

Small cottage for rent , reasonable rates , office has a picture window on to the Village Pond. Apply at any local Estate agents.

Printed in Great Britain
by Amazon